GAY SEX TALES

EXPLICIT DIRTY EROTICA SHORT STORIES

CHANEY KEES

plicit Press
Erotica Fiction

CHAPTER 1

LICENSE AND REGISTRATION PLEASE... (IS THERE A PROBLEM OFFICER?)

GORDY CLOSES the laptop on his lap as he pulls over. But he knows that he's been spotted. He puts it on the passenger seat and then undoes his seatbelt. Just as he rolls down his window for the officer tapping on the glass his phone rings. Instinctively he takes the call. The officer watches in disbelief as Gordy finishes a ten-minute conversation.

When he puts the phone down, he meets the stern look of Officer James. He assumes that his first name is Lyle, which it is, even though the nametag just has his initial. He calls him Lyle, which makes the cop soften a little. But as duty demands, he informs Gordy of his offenses and then pulls out his pad to start with the ticket write-up. Gordy isn't even sure how, or if, he wants to talk his way out of this one.

Then Lyle looks around the inside of the car, checking out the driver more than anything else though. He points out the severity of the offenses and lets Gordy know just how much it will cost him in traffic fines. Gordy really isn't worried about the money. He makes enough of it. But he picks up on the suggestive tone the officer has and wonders what it is he is suggesting as an alternative to the ticket.

Lyle rubs over his dick and watches Gordy's eyes on his hand as it moves up and down on his meat. Lyle's cock gets bigger and longer and Gordy cannot help but stare. He isn't sure if he is reading the situation properly so he doesn't make a move. Then Lyle goes around to the passenger side of the vehicle. He waits for a moment until Gordy figures it out and reaches over to unlock it. A moment later, Lyle is sitting in the seat next to him.

Without asking, Lyle reaches between Gordy's legs and strokes his cock. It isn't hard yet. Gordy doesn't allow himself to get hard until he is assured of satisfaction. He isn't sure yet. But Lyle isn't giving up, rubbing harder and harder over Gordy's bulge. Finally, it starts to respond, and the dick that Lyle is playing with starts to extend.

It is incredibly difficult for Lyle to get Gordy's dick out. So he reaches over and pulls the lever that reclines the driver's seat. Then he manages easily to undo the belt, button, and then the zip of Gordy's pants. He reaches into his underwear and pulls out the cock that is now stretched quite impressively. He leans over and puts the tip of Gordy's cock in his mouth. Sucking on just the first part of his dick, Lyle gets Gordy to a full erection.

A good bit of oral in the middle of the day is never a bad thing. So Gordy thrusts his cock into Lyle's mouth as the cop enjoys sucking it. Lyle's mouth slides all the way to the base of his meat and then he moves his head around and around so that Gordy's dick is stirring the contents of his mouth like an erotic soup. The mouth is hot, perfect, wet, and thankfully fucking deep.

Gordy plays with his own balls. Then he rubs Lyle's head and also his back. This is a killer fucking blowjob. Lyle takes to his cock with the kind of enthusiasm that any man would find flattering. Gordy can't resist fucking the traffic officer's mouth harder, payback for all the other cops who've stopped him without having the decency to suck his dick.

Lyle sucks on this impressive dick until Gordy fills his mouth with hot cum. It seems to be over too quickly and Gordy is a little disappointed. But he is also satisfied, watching as Lyle licks his dick clean after swallowing his seed. He checks his watch to see if he hasn't eaten too much into his day, waiting for the officer to make a modest escape from his vehicle.

But when Lyle recovers into a seated position, he doesn't go for the door. Instead, he pulls out his own dick, fumbles in his pocket, pulls out a condom, and slides it down his shaft. Gordy didn't expect this. He wants to object, but can't, given that he has had an orgasm. It's only fair that the officer has one too. But if he is going to be fucked it means that he is going to have to make a detour home, or to the gym, to shower before his next meeting.

Lyle turns him over and then exposes his ass. Gordy feels a chill as his bum is now open and exposed. He rolls the windows back up, the breeze a little intrusive. Lyle parts his cheeks and murmurs with pleasure as he looks at the tiny hole. He gives it a kiss before spitting into it. Then he fingers it with two fingers to test the tension. It gives way to his fingers easily.

After positioning himself on top of Gordy, he goes into him with his dick. Even before he is all the way inside, he is fucking Gordy hard. This is some hot fucking ass. Gordy holds onto the backrest of his seat and braces himself for this exciting thrusting coming from above. Lyle obviously loves fucking ass.

He goes in and out and then in wide circles as he wants

to feel every part of Gordy's ass with his cock. It isn't long before Gordy is thoroughly enjoying being fucked by Lyle. Nothing beats being fucked by someone who knows how to handle ass. Lyle's thrusts are perfect. Each one is different but complete. He works every corner or this offender's asshole using every part of his cock.

After he's been going at it for a while, it is clear that Lyle is enjoying it too much to cum just yet. Gordy is having a great time too so he isn't complaining. Lyle pulls his dick out and then pulls the seat back up so that he is now kneeling behind Gordy, who is still hugging the backrest of the chair. He drives his cock into his ass again in this position and hugs the seat and Gordy at the same time, fucking him good and solid with no sign of relenting.

He moves his waist from side to side. Gordy moves his ass back and forth, practically fucking his car seat. Then Lyle is moving again in wide circles. Still, Gordy pushes his ass onto Lyle's cock and then away. They perfect this dance, rhythms in perfect sync. But there is still no sign that Gordy is about to be given a break anytime soon since Lyle is clearly nowhere near cumming.

After a while, in this position, Lyle assures Gordy that he has a whole lot more in him, but that he understands that Gordy probably has somewhere to be so he'll finish up. He pulls his cock from Gordy again and then gets back in the passenger seat. He reclines it and then relaxes onto his back while holding his cock up. He encourages Gordy to mount. This isn't possible unless Gordy removes his trousers, which he does reluctantly.

He gets on top of Lyle, facing away from him. Lyle's dick goes into him easily and Gordy rests his head on the dash as he starts to ride the cock planted inside him. His ass is starting to burn, the thickness of Lyle's cock taking its toll.

But he goes for it with gusto, following the instructions from Lyle to ride him round and round.

After a minute, Lyle is lifting and lowering Gordy on his dick. This cop is pretty strong because he manages to lift Gordy quite high up on his shaft and lower him with incredible control back down. He fucks him harder and harder, moving him vigorously up and down and around on his dick. Soon enough Gordy doesn't have to do anything as Lyle takes full control. But still, there is no sign of Lyle having a climax, despite Gordy already leaking a little from his own dick, which is already hard again.

Then Lyle lifts Gordy all the way off his cock again and Gordy is frustrated. This cunt is enjoying the shit out of his asshole, clearly. But he is really pushing it and enjoying it too much. He is asked to turn to face Lyle and sit on his dick again. Gordy obeys. He has already fallen foul of the law once today. He may as well just do as he's told. Now Lyle is stroking Gordy's erection as Gordy rides his dick. He is trying without saying it to get the officer to shoot but it is clear that this is not going to be up to him. He just has to relax into the fucking and let Lyle satisfy himself. It seems that Lyle will satisfy Gordy too as he wets his palm with spit and then works the full length of Gordy's cock with his wet hand.

He moves up and down the shaft slowly, begging Gordy to grind in slow steady circles on his cock. He begs Gordy not to change a thing once he reaches the perfect pace and intensity. Now there is hope. Now Gordy feels that maybe this is indeed the final stretch. He wishes to himself that when the hand on his cock milks it to completion he shoots a massive load on Lyle's uniform just as a final fuck you to the law. But Lyle is no amateur.

He moves up and down on Gordy's cock at a measured

pace. Then he stops on his head and rubs the dome aggressively, pulling him back from his climax each time he gets too close. Then he goes back onto the shaft and works him back up toward the climax. But Gordy doesn't change his grinding, Lyle continuously begging him to keep it steady.

Finally, Gordy can't take this and begs Lyle to let him cum. Lyle holds on just a little. He doesn't move his cock at all now as Gordy is working it perfectly. The ass enveloping his dick makes Lyle extremely happy, his cock firm and ready to blow. It takes a further ten minutes before Lyle's orgasm is in full swing.

As he starts to cum, he moves up and down on Gordy's shaft and brings him to his own climax. Gordy starts to shoot his load; a load caught by Lyle's other hand over his head. Lyle keeps on stroking up and down Gordy's shaft until he has completely milked his dick. Gordy too keeps grinding in small circles on the dick inside his ass until it is clear on Lyle's face that he is satisfied.

To his surprise, Lyle then proceeds to lick all Gordy's semen off his hands. He takes every drop of it into his mouth and then swallows it with a smile. Then Gordy eases his ass up and off Lyle's dick, which he finds to be still rock solid despite his orgasm. There is no way for Gordy to hide the fact that he is incredibly impressed with this man.

Lyle gets the condom off himself while Gordy gets his own pants back on. Then he takes some wipes from his glove compartment and gives them to Lyle, who finishes cleaning himself. As he starts to run a wipe up and down his shaft, his erection seems determined not to go anywhere.

Gordy goes onto the tool with his mouth and mimics the pace he had with his ass, using his mouth. Lyle is incredibly grateful, lying there and letting his cock be sucked.

Gordy gives Lyle a languid, patient blowjob. He owes

him this much. It takes long again for Lyle to give any signs that he is close to cumming. But when it is clear that he is on the way to another blow Gordy keeps going. Eventually, Lyle shoots another, massive, sticky load into Gordy's mouth. Gordy too is a swallower and takes every drop of Lyle's jizz into himself. The men pull themselves together and after a stern warning, Lyle sends Gordy on his merry, satisfied way...

CHAPTER 2

SECURITY? (MOVING UP!)

THE TWO MEN are sweaty by the time they pop open their beers. Rick had tried to move as much of his stuff up to his new apartment by himself as possible. But eventually, the boxes just got too big. Fortunately, Carl, the resident security guy, wasn't too busy to help.

Both men are hot. They are young, muscled, and horny. They sit topless in Rick's new lounge, the sofa fortunately already there and one of the only things that aren't wrapped in a box. Rick and Carl sit side by side and chat easily about the building and Carl's job and his life and other shit. Rick tells Carl a little about himself too. Before they realize it, they've had three beers and the sun has started to go down.

Rick gets up to go and turns on a light. He says this out loud. Carl pulls him back onto the sofa in the dark. Carl's grip on Rick's arm is firm. It also lingers even after Rick is sitting back down.

Carl goes in for a kiss before he can even see clearly where Rick's mouth is. He doesn't even know if Rick is open to this.

When Carl can't find Rick's mouth, he settles his lips on

his neck. What starts off as kissing becomes biting. This is just what Rick likes, aggressive masculine contact. Carl runs his lips up and down on Rick's neck between his bites. With their beers put down, Rick gets on the couch completely and Carl gets on top of him. Rick takes his shorts off and then gets Carl's jeans off. In their underwear, they find each other's lips at last. The kiss is hard and aggressive. It is deeply masculine and what both men like. They move their tongues into each other's mouths interchangeably, this passion growing their cocks considerably.

Rick gets his and Carl's underwear off while they continue kissing. As soon as their dicks touch, Carl knows that the new tenant is open to what he has spontaneously put on offer. There is just the matter of whether or not Rick is open to being fucked, or if it's going to be the other way around.

He goes down Rick's chest with his lips and then swallows his dick. He makes it all the way down Rick's shaft. Then he moves his mouth up and nibbles on Rick's tip for a while before swallowing his cock completely again. Rick runs his fingers through Carl's hair for a bit and then pushes him hard down on his dick.

It's a beautiful blowjob. Carl really knows how to suck a dick. Rick allows himself to just let his cock be eaten. Carl isn't complaining, sucking long, hard and deep. But he still has the lingering question, wanting to know whether or not he is going to be able to get some ass here tonight. He moves around so that he can drop his cock into Rick's mouth so that they can suck each other off at the same time, just in case this is as far as Rick is prepared to go.

But then Carl decides not to be a pussy. He pulls his cock from Rick's mouth and then gets his own cock free. Then he encourages Rick onto his stomach. He allows himself to move until Carl is running his hands over his back and onto his ass. The muscle is firm, warm, and inviting. Carl wants to put a finger into his asshole. But he goes in with his tongue first to test Rick's response.

He takes a deep line, sending his tongue onto the hole he can't see and flicking fast over it. Then he licks it harder and tries to get his tongue inside Rick. The hole is tight, but not impenetrable. After a few more licks he gets into the tight hole, finding it hot and inviting. He wants his cock inside Rick now more than ever.

Rick raises his ass as Carl's tongue digs deeper into it. This increases his optimism as he realizes that this man has definitely been fucked before. So he gives him as much of a tongue slobbering as he can before he can't take it anymore and needs to start fucking.

He feels again around Rick's asshole, stirring the spit around that he left there. Then he goes in with his finger, finding the ass still tight, but a lot more receptive. He adds another finger and Rick groans. When Rick feels a third finger inside his asshole, he takes a deep breath. He hasn't been fucked in a while. But he isn't about to let Carl know this. The security guard is too hot to pass up.

Carl fingers Rick persistently until Rick relaxes at last into the sensation. He keeps fingering while aligning himself on top of Rick. Then he eases his fingers out of him and puts some spit on his cock, making sure that the tip of his dick is lathered sufficiently. Carl places the tip inside Rick's hole and then pauses. He fucks Rick slowly with about three inches of his cock until it starts to slide in easily.

Then Carl places his hands on Rick's head and starts to massage his scalp as he lowers a little more of his dick into him. Rick's hole wraps tightly around Carl's cock, a natural reflex. But Rick takes another deep breath and raises his ass against the full weight of the man on top of him. Carl goes deeper but is careful not to invade too quickly.

With help from Rick Carl is finally all up in Rick's boot. He moves from massaging his head to his neck and shoulders so that Rick relaxes into the sensations of being fucked. Because Carl manages slow and steady thrusts it isn't long before Rick is grinding hard against Carl's dick, and Carl knows that he now has permission to fuck this man like a man.

Rick buries his face in the sofa as Carl builds momentum. Understanding the dynamic of being fucked, Carl leaves Rick in this hiding place for a while as he continues to bury his cock deep inside this asshole that is everything his cock had ordered. Then he slides an arm under Rick's neck in a mock chokehold and turns Rick's face to the side. Carl finds the side of Rick's face with his lips before finding his mouth. He kisses Rick deeply, fucks him deeply, and then shoots a highly anticipated load of hot jizz into his asshole before slumping, satisfied on top of him.

When his dick is finally empty and flaccid Carl starts to make a slow exit. Even soft Carl's cock is thick and long. It takes a while until the head of his meat finally slips from the generous manhole. Rick exhales loud when he is finally free of the security guard's powerful baton.

Carl puts his tongue on Rick's hole again, and then inside it. He licks it tenderly, almost apologetically until Rick has recovered. Then they are facing each other and their mouths are locked. Rick's erection is rubbing against Carl and it soon becomes clear that he needs to shoot a load too. But Carl has also not been fucked in a while. In fact, Carl has only ever let himself be fucked once before, many years ago. He goes onto Rick's cock with his mouth, hoping that Rick will be satisfied shooting his load into his mouth.

But then Rick has Carl on his back. He raises the guard's legs and finds his asshole with his mouth. Rick isn't surprised by the hair he finds there, Carl being quite hairy all over. He licks gently for a while until he senses that this is more of an uncomfortable tickle for this man who hasn't had his ass played with properly. So Rick starts to lick the hairy hole hard. Soon enough Carl is groaning ecstatically.

It's not easy getting his tongue into the man-cunt. Carl is locked shut, tight and unyielding. Rick holds both Carl's legs over his chest so that his ass is a little higher in the air. He drops large blobs of spit onto Carl's ass, missing occasionally and spitting directly onto his bum. He uses his free hand to smear the spit towards the hole and then onto it. Carl panics and reveals that he's only ever been fucked once. Rick assures him that he just wants to play a little and that Carl must relax. This is of course easier said than done.

Rick rubs Carl's asshole hard with the tip of his index finger. He keeps rubbing until Carl moans, processing the pleasure even though he is still anxious about the possibility. Then the tip of the finger makes an entry and Carl winces. Rick drives the rest of the finger into Carl, telling him to breathe. Before Carl can even process breathing, he is being fingered hard and fast with this thick index. Rick's cock wants in now and so he is going to try and loosen Carl up quickly.

More spit finds Carl's asshole and the finger moves easier in and out of him. Rick informs Carl that he is going to try two fingers and after a minute Carl says he should go for it. Rick shoots four fingers into Carl instead and Carl's legs push against the arm holding them down. But Rick is as strong as him, their power matched. He holds Carl in position and fingers him for as long as he needs to so that Carl's ass isn't squashing his four fingers with his muscled ring.

Rick comes up high and removes his fingers from Carl so that he can place his hands on his dick and point it into the tight circle he has intimate intentions towards. He drops his rock-hard cock into Carl completely in one go. Again, Carl winces, too late because Rick's cock is lodged deep inside him already. Rick moves Carl's legs so that they are against his own chest. Then Rick goes down on Carl so that the man's powerful, toned, hairy legs are sandwiched between their chests. He slides his cock out just a little and then makes a full thrust back into Carl.

There is no time to allow Carl to adjust. Each stroke feels like the first so every time Rick stops fucking, Carl feels like the whole thing is just starting again. This sends signals to his asshole to tighten and attempt by all means to eject the cock inside it. So Rick gathers all his strength and just fucks his moving assistant harder and harder.

Carl is moving around wildly under Rick. But he isn't getting very far, impaled to the couch by Rick's fourteen inches and held down by Rick's hands on his shoulders. Rick is really fucking him with all that he's got, begging him to take it, to just stop fighting it, to give in to his cock. Carl knows that this is what will make it easier, and speed up the journey to enjoyment. But being able to take cock in your ass is something that you perfect with practice. He hasn't had much.

Rick doesn't let up, keeping Carl where he is while sending thrust upon powerful thrust into him. It takes thirty determined minutes and a whole lot of sweat before Rick can feel that Carl is surrendering. When he does, his cock goes all the way into Carl and all the way out easily. Rick is able to make a full exit and then shoot powerfully all the way back in. He does this a few times, confirming for Carl that his hole is fuck-worthy now. Carl registers for the first time that sensation that has so many men primed about taking boners into their rear ends.

It takes another thirty minutes before Rick shoots his load into Carl. He gets Carl onto his side without removing his hard dick from him. Rick stays inside Carl, fucking him in slower strokes until he has another orgasm. Carl has one too, but only because Rick beats his meat for the duration of the fucking. Now that they are both opened up and ready, they can have another beer before really taking both their asses and cocks to task for the rest of the evening...

CHAPTER 3

WRESTLE MANIA (CONTACT SPORTS...)

ALI IS a hot Arab from Dubai who got to Harvard on a sports scholarship. Who would have thought that wrestling was so big in Dubai? In fact, twenty-two-year-old Ali is the captain of the college team. It is for this reason that Quade has asked him for this extra session so that he can get the hang of this sport that he has decided to do, rather than the more intense high-pressure team sports on offer.

The gym is dark for the most part when Quade arrives. He thinks he is the only one in the hall. But then he catches a shadow on the bleachers. Ali is having a drink from his water bottle. When Quade gets closer to him, Ali comes down the bleachers and drags the mat to the far corner of the hall. It's out of view from the door, which has two glass panels that would make them visible from the outside should someone look in, if they were to leave the mat in the center of the room. Quade assumes that this is to make him more comfortable, being such a novice.

They get down to their wrestling gear. There is a need for them to protect their cocks with jockstraps but Ali says this is not necessary for this practice session, which Ali says will be light. Quade doesn't argue and leaves his pad in his bag. They start with simple sparring, Ali explaining the various holds to Quade.

Ali isn't shy about getting his hands high up the inside of Quade's leg, sometimes stopping short of his cock, but often not. Quade doesn't pay this too much mind until a stray finger finds his balls and stays there, rubbing the surface of his nuts over his tight gear. He breaks away and gives Ali a questioning look. Ali is unfazed, coming back in and grabbing a firm hold of Quade's ball before raising him off the floor and dropping him back on the mat.

Ali is on top of him now, his hands again running up the inside of his legs and finding his cock. He doesn't just graze his balls now, but places his hand over Quade's thick cock, giving it a firm squeeze before rubbing it up and down the surface of the shaft. Ali traces the line of Quade's cock and then circles over the head of the massive dick. When Quade is again giving him a questioning look, Ali compliments him on his impressive meat and then guides Quade's hand onto his own cock. Quade is shocked to find that the Arab has a massive boner straining inside his leotard.

But he can't resist giving Ali's erection a squeeze. It too is some impressive cock. Ali moves Quade's hand up and down on his shaft. He makes contact with Quade's cock again and is surprised that it is still soft. Ali pulls him into the corner of the room and then around to the back of the bleachers. They get to the part under the chairs where they can stand. But Ali doesn't stand for long.

He gets on his knees and sends a hand under the bottom of Quade's gear, finds his dick, and gently pulls it out of the elastic. He puts it in his mouth and starts sucking on the bulging head slowly. He goes for most of the shaft and then encounters the stretch resistance of the fabric. He works on it with his hand so that the leotard is pulled to one side of Quade's balls and cock now hangs freely. Ali's mouth now manages to fill with all of the thick softness hanging in front of him.

Even though his dick is still soft, Quade makes the kind of sounds that let Ali know that he is really enjoying it. Ali wets his fingers and lathers the balls at the base of the dick he is sucking. Now his cock starts to swell, and Ali is happy as his mouth is stretched further to the back when Quade grows a full erection. Now he sucks this hardness with as much vigor as he had shown on the wrestling mat.

They get onto the floor and position themselves so that they are facing each other's cocks. Quade gets Ali's dick free and into his mouth too. They suck on each other's meat slowly, enjoying the taste of cock in their mouths. They manage because of their similar heights to get each other's dicks all the way into their mouths, sucking on the whole tool despite their lengths. Ali is really pleased with himself, and with the fact that he read Quade correctly.

He doesn't want Quade to cum yet, in case it makes him awkward afterward. There are a few more things that Ali would like to try. So he gets Quade as close to exploding as possible and then takes his mouth off his dick. Quade keeps sucking though, not sure what Ali has in mind. Ali is quick to let him know though. After taking his cock from Quade's mouth Ali repositions himself so they are facing each other. He takes Quade's hand and guides it under his gear so that it is on his ass. He moves Quade to his asshole and Quade knows what he wants. He feels around for Ali's asshole and then pushes his finger into it. The finger slides in easily. Ali grunts as Quade digs his finger deep into Ali's hole.

He keeps fingering him while Ali holds his cock and moves his hand up and down on it. Ali is careful not to stroke Quade's cock too quickly in case he cums. But Quade has no intention of cumming, not now that he has felt the beautiful hole that is between Ali's cheeks. He wants it now, and he will have it. Ali started this, but Quade will end it.

Ali turns to face his ass to Quade. He pulls the fabric covering the ass and slides his cock underneath it. Then he finds the valley and settles his dick between them. He pulls him closer to him so that the length of his shaft is snug between Ali's firm butt cheeks. Ali is already begging him to get in there. Ali doesn't wait long.

After grinding up and down on Ali's crack, Quade makes a sudden entry into the hole he was fingering just a minute ago. He goes in and holds Ali to him so that he doesn't try to get away. Ali obviously underestimated Quade's cock. With a firm hand on his side, Quade pulls Ali all the way onto his dick until he is all the way inside his asshole. Ali moans like a bitch. Quade loves it.

Ali is pushed away a little so that some of Quade is out of him again just a little. Then he pulls him closer again so that more of his dick moves into Ali again. Over and over again, Ali is pushed back and forth on Quade's cock, with no movement from Quade just yet. Ali is in heaven. This isn't the kind of response he expected from the muscular wrestler, but Quade and his cock are not complaining at all.

Then Quade pushes Ali away just so that his tip is still inside his ass. Then he follows him with his cock so that Ali is on his stomach and Quade is on top of him. Then Ali moans loudly as cock is dropped swiftly and completely into his asshole. Then Quade lifts his dick up out of Ali a little before plunging into him again. Quade has Ali's legs gripped firmly between his own.

Quade gets Ali into a firm hold as he thrusts hard into

him repeatedly. His dick fills the tight hole completely and Ali has no way of escaping this dick. It seems that Quade has a few wrestling skills of his own. His cock now launches a massive attack on the Arabian asshole. This is one of Quade's favorite positions and he could fuck Ali like this forever.

Then he sends his legs between Ali's so that Ali spreads wide. Ali wriggles a little as though he is trying to escape Quade's hold. But Quade is not letting him go. He drives his dick into him hard. Quade pulls Ali down, dragging him on the floor as he continues to feed Ali more and more of his dick, harder and harder. Quade's thrusting is relentless. Quade proves his strength again when he brings Ali up to his knees and fucks him like this for a minute before standing up, taking Ali with him. He has Ali firmly hooked to himself on his dick. He carries Ali toward the bleachers and Ali takes hold as soon as he can reach. He holds himself tight against the wood while Quade keeps his wood moving steadily in and out of Ali's manhole.

The tight elastic of what they're wearing is starting to grate against Quade's cock. This feeling makes him feel like he is being kept from really going for it. He takes the top part of his own leotard off until it is around his waist. He does the same to Ali's. Then he pulls his cock from Ali's ass and then pulls his gear down under his ass. Quade gets Ali's all the way down to his ankles. Ali senses now that this is game over, and totally naked like this, there will be no stopping this beast that he has awakened.

It takes some effort to get back into Ali's ass since it is so muscled that it closes tight quickly. But Quade doesn't take no for an answer and he is soon thrusting his full length back into Ali. This is some seriously firm ass, just the way Quade likes it. He drives over and over into it, pulling more and more moaning from Ali. Quade is also pulling on Ali's dick now as he sends powerful strokes into him from his twelve inches.

Quade pulls Ali away from his perch and lets him bend forward. Ali reaches the floor forming a V at his waist. His ass is on fire as Quade fucks him hard, forcing him to move forward as though he was trying to crawl away from the cock inside him. But this is some seriously determined dick and Ali soon accepts that he will not be going anywhere until Quade is done. Ali hadn't banked on Quade being so filled with sexual stamina.

Then Quade is on his knees again behind Ali. He coaches the Arab forward until Ali is able to place his hands on the wall. With nowhere to move forward now, Quade can dig all the way inside Ali and work himself up to the end of this practice session. Ali has one hand on the wall, masturbating with the other hand so that he can cum with Quade. He can feel the pumping inside his ass, the throbbing of the cock that is a reliable signal that Quade is almost done.

Ali manages to move his ass in circles now as Quade thrusts harder. His own dick is almost ready to spray a sticky coat onto the floor. Ali isn't going to hold himself back. He is going to cum as soon as he is ready, hoping that Quade will cum soon after. Ali's hand is now firm on his own dick and he is pulling on his cock hard. He is so close that even the dick ripping his ass apart is a bit of a blur now.

But Quade isn't about to become a total blur. He goes into him even harder, pulling Ali from his orgasmic lull. Over and over, Quade reminds Ali with his cock that he is being fucked. Ali can only keep working on his own cock now since Quade is taking care of his, Ali's ass proving to be an incredible sparring partner. They are both all about their own orgasms now as the fucking becomes furious and Ali's wanking gains momentum. The orgasms are loud and for the most part simultaneous. Ali guides the removal of the dick from his ass, Quade being a gentleman and letting him. They sit on the cold floor and recover before playing with each other's cocks a little bit more. They get dressed again and to Quade's surprise, Ali insists on finishing up with their practice.

CHAPTER 4

TREE-HOUSE NOSTALGIA!
(THE HIDEAWAY...)

THE TREEHOUSE LOOKS like it did when they were kids. Rob is home for the weekend and was surprised when he bumped into his childhood buddy, Tino, at the liquor store. They decided to take their beers back to Rob's house so that they can drink in the old hideaway and catch up about their experiences at their respective colleges.

It is easy to get caught up in the memories of the past. They drink and laugh, remembering everything from broken arms, first and last cigarettes, first beers, sleepovers, and erections. Tino had an impressive cock, even when he was younger, Rob remembers. Rob isn't ungifted himself, something that Tino remembers from the many times they played cock archery, seeing who had the best shooting range when they were teenagers.

This memory is the one that seems to occupy the pair most, discussing all the other guys who are not here right now. They remember the game, the cocks, the aim, the cleanup. It was really the purest abandon of youth. The beers make it easier and easier for the pair to discuss cock. After a few more beers, it is easy to discuss their own cocks.

The cushions on the floor are clean, thanks to Rob's mom taking in a foster kid who's all but taken over the treehouse. So they recline comfortably on the soft pads so that they can drink and chat comfortably. It's pretty warm tonight, so they are both in shorts and college shirts. Americans have such ridiculous college pride. Rob and Tino lie next to each other, closer than they have in years. They remember each other's dicks fondly.

Then Rob reaches for Tino's hand, which is resting on his dick. Tino isn't sure for a second what his friend is doing, but then he moves his hand so that Rob's hand is on his dick directly, except for his shorts. Tino has a semi-hard-on, and Rob is happy with the response he has already. His own dick gets harder as Tino stiffens considerably.

They take another sip of their beers while Rob moves his hands more firmly over his friend's dick. It's not an uncomfortable moment. They've touched each other's cocks before. They've made each other cum before. But now they've grown up. Now it can't just be put down to a game. Both men down the beer they're drinking and open another one.

After this beer, both Rob and Tino are rubbing each other's erections. It soon becomes clear that the shorts are in the way. But both of them take their shirts off first. They have another beer, discussing college but wanting to touch each other. Tino remembers the latch on the trapdoor that will keep any midnight intruders out. He secures it and then takes off his shorts. Rob is suddenly unsure, but Tino is already taking off Rob's shorts. They lie naked on the cushions looking at each other's grown-up bodies, sipping on their beers.

Rob reaches for Tino's dick again and feathers his buddy's shaft with his fingertips. He moves up and down the length and really appreciates how his bud has grown. Then Tino is stroking his cock. He is happy that his dick has caught up to Rob's in adulthood. Rob has always had a huge cock. This was a bone of contention that saw them all jealous of Rob for a long time growing up.

They both get onto their backs and move in closer to each other. They look up through the skylight that allows them to watch the night sky or the rainfall. Still, they are touching each other's cocks, moving up from the base of their dicks to the tip, and then onto their balls. Both of them have significantly sized balls. Tino has a gentler squeeze on Rob's sack, Rob a little firmer. Thankfully, they are both comfortable enough with each other to let the other know how hard or soft to squeeze.

The friends are very relaxed in each other's company, even in each other's nakedness now. There is increased touching, not just of cock now but also up and down chests and on each other's nipples. Then they are touching each other's necks and faces more intimately than they've ever done before. There is intense chemistry between them now that was never entertained before. Another beer and the chemistry is something that they are prepared to explore now.

Then they are kissing. Both Rob and Tino have thick, full lips and hot tongues. They explore each other's mouths intensely, coming in closer so that as much of their bodies are touching. Their dicks rub up and down together and the fire builds to an inferno inside them. Rob is completely lost in the moment now while Tino is a little more focused, taking a more assertive approach as it becomes clear that Rob is submitting to his touch.

Tino gets on top of Rob. He reaches between them and adjusts their cocks so that they are connected along the shafts and at the heads. Then Tino urges Rob's legs apart so that even their balls are settled snuggly together on one another's. There is no more comfortable position for them to be in at this moment.

Their kissing intensifies. Tino explores Rob's lips with an almost fervor. Then he gets back up to his face and sucks up the beer on Rob's tongue. Rob's eyes are closed but Tino is watching his face. This is an unexpected treat for him, and he wants to take in everything about this moment. Rob doesn't mind just losing himself in the moment.

Tino's hands move up and down the sides of Rob's body while he continues to kiss him. He settles his fingers on his head and then bends it back a little so that he can taste the front of Rob's neck. Tino is clearly a lover. He has no urgency to fuck and is determined to make sure that this is a sensual experience for Rob, who he now wants to make love to. But they've never played all the way before so he can't rush it.

When he has his mouth on Rob's nipples, it is clear that Rob likes this. So he lingers on the thick pink nipples so that he offers as much pleasure as possible. He is pulling on Rob's nuts at the same time, gently tugging the massive orbs while biting into his nipples. Rob is in heaven. He parts his legs far and bends his knees.

Tino sees the invitation and goes past Rob's cock, taking his balls into his mouth. He sucks on the nuts as gently as he was sucking on the nipples. He bites into Rob's sack gently until his teeth make contact with Rob's balls. Then he is sucking on the orbs again. After a while, he lifts the sack with his forehead, and Tino's tongue is lapping up the sweat on the tender spot between Rob's asshole and his balls.

As he works up again onto Rob's cock Tino goes into his friend's ass with his finger. He slips just a little bit of his finger into him and as Rob winces, Tino stops. He almost bends over double between Rob's legs so that he can suck his cock while gently stretching his ass with just the tip of his index finger. As he keeps going, Rob's ass loosens nicely, so that Tino is now fingering him all the way inside with his finger.

By the time Tino is kissing Rob on his lips again, he is fingering him with two fingers, Rob resting on a cushion placed strategically under his back, his legs lifted to the side and held there by his own hands on his knees. He is subconsciously doing all the right things to make it easy for Tino to keep making him feel good.

Tino nibbles on his ear, making Rob almost shiver with pleasure. He pulls out his fingers slowly and rubs Rob on the inside of his thigh, firmly, squeezing occasionally. Tino's cock is now underneath Rob, close enough to his asshole for Rob to feel a little nervous now. But Tino has been so patient and attentive that he will allow him into his ass come hell or high water. Tino is the perfect first time for this anyway.

Rob feels the cock against the hole that he has never had a dick inside of before. He doesn't know how to let him into his ass so he has to just trust Tino to do what needs to be done to get inside there. He stiffens more than he would have liked as Tino manages to get his head into his asshole. It's an incredible sense of intrusion and he isn't sure where to move. Tino holds him firmly so that the tip doesn't slip out. He sends his tongue into Rob's ear, something that distracts him so much that more cock gets into him.

Tino checks that Rob is okay as he moves deeper into him. Rob is honest about not being totally in it yet but is also quick to let Tino know that he wants him all the way inside. Tino goes at it gently, slowly filling Rob's ass with his dick. The thick meat drags hard along the side of Rob's ring, but Tino's dick is strong enough to push through the resistance. His erection is so powerful that he doesn't need to force himself in too fast. His cock has no intention of losing any of its rigidity.

When Tino is finally all the way inside Rob he exhales with a huge sigh of relief. He tells Rob that he is all up in there and that he can relax now. Rob tries, but as soon Tino starts to move his cock out a little to facilitate a thrust, the drag is almost too intense for Rob. So again, Tino drives his cock all the way inside him and settles there. After a minute, he tries again, and again he needs to go all the way back in because Rob is having trouble adjusting to the withdrawal.

Then Tino has an idea. He removes his dick from Rob slowly until he is all the way out. Then he positions Rob on his side so that he is comfortable enough with a beer in his hand. Then they start drinking another beer, Tino teasing Rob's hole with his cock for a while and then slowly reintroducing it to the asshole that he hungers for. Soon enough he is inside Rob again.

They chat, joke, and laugh as Tino's dick stretches Rob. Then he starts to move out slowly while continuing the conversation. Rob responds to what he is saying, letting him know when he needs to go easy on the thrusting. Tino is really not about to hurry anything so he sips on his beer and then starts to give Rob a massage after warming his hands by rubbing them together. Finally, he is thrusting steadily in and out of Rob's ass, Rob grunting from the pleasure delivered into him with each stroke.

Now that Tino has him loose and taking it, he gets him

back on his back, raised up again on the cushion, and really starts to make love to him. He comes down on Rob with his face and kisses him while lifting his dick high out and then dropping it lower and lower into Rob. This is a moment that Tino has secretly longed for years. This is a moment that Rob didn't even know he longed for until now. Everything seems to come together perfectly as the two of them connect in the most beautiful way.

Tino takes his time with Rob, exploring every position available to the two men. When he feels like he is about to cum, he pulls his cock slowly from Robb and lies down next to him. He takes Rob's dick in his hand, Rob taking his. The two of them slowly stroke each other's dicks as they used to do, until they have intense orgasms, spraying semen all over themselves and each other. This is the kind of situation that really makes their treehouse the perfect hideaway, even after all these years...

CHAPTER 5

THE CABLE GUY

THE SIGHT OF NINETEEN-YEAR-OLD RUSSELL, lean and toned in his tight blue jeans and a white vest, immediately stir every lust inside Jeff. Jeff himself isn't unattractive, an athletic forty-five. The heat outside has both men sweating, despite the living room being generously soaked by the air- conditioning. Russell is already halfway through his third soda, the cable he came to fix practically fixed. It doesn't take long for Jeff to realize that he doesn't want Russell to leave, not until they've explored a fantasy that's been playing in his head since he opened the door for the young man a couple of hours earlier.

Taking the glass from him, Jeff lets his hand settle on Russell's for a moment longer than it needs to. He places the glass on the nearest available surface and then turns immediately to face Russell again. There is tension in Russell's eyes that makes Jeff offer him a stronger drink.

Russell is quick to accept, and even quicker to drink it. Despite the obvious intention hanging in the room, Russell doesn't move, at least not away. He shuffles instead on the spot, downing a second courage-firming drink.

Before the moment is lost Jeff lets his hand rest on Russell's crotch. He gives the soft cock under the denim a firm squeeze. Russell's eyes are on Jeff's, then on his crotch. He watches as his cock gets squeezed gently, repeatedly. Under the firm grip of Jeff's large hands, Russell's cock begins to grow. His erection pushes against the denim, craving the touch that brought it to life. This surprises Russell visibly. He's obviously never been touched by a man this way. But by the bulge in his pants, it's clear that it isn't something he hasn't thought about, and it's definitely something that he likes.

Nervously Russell does the same, his hand on Jeff's cock. Jeff's meat is already hard, ready to be handled. But he knows he can't rush this, not with a newbie. He lets Russell acquaint himself with his cock, its thickness, its length, and its curve of it. His fingers keep teasing the top of Jeff's jeans, but Russell is nowhere near ready for what this will mean. So he just keeps his fingers moving over Jeff's tool, getting more and more comfortable with the dick as the moments elapse. Jeff eyes Russell's pretty mouth, blood-red lips against his pale face, and his patience wears thin.

For a moment, they struggle with each other's buttons and are both defeated. Each man tackles his own pants, jeans buttons were undone, jeans pulled down to their knees and then off. Both stand in their underwear, Jeff in Klein's and Russell in checkered boxers. Both men sport massive erections, Russell's tool pointing forward, threatening to escape through the slit in the front of his shorts. Jeff's erection points in the direction of the earth, his heavy cock almost *falling* towards the ground. They don't stand staring for too long.

Jeff pulls down Russell's boxers as he gets down on his haunches. As Russell lifts his legs out of his shorts, Jeff is already wrapping his mouth around his cock. He takes the uncircumcised cock into his mouth completely, Russell releasing a series of what can only be described as whimpers. Either he's never had his cock sucked before or he's never had his cock swallowed completely before, which is Jeff's world is the equivalent of never having had your cock sucked. Russell is deep-throated for the first time, Jeff enjoying his role as a teacher almost as much as Russell is enjoying being schooled.

Russell's cock is released before he succumbs to the urge to shoot off inside Jeff's mouth. Experience has taught Jeff that if you let a first-timer cum before you've done everything you wish done, your chances of anything more are virtually zero. If Russell shoots a load now, there is no chance that he will have the balls to attend to Jeff's cock, the only thing on his mind being to create as much distance between him and the experience. So Jeff frees the amateur cock from his mouth and pulls his own underwear off as he stands. His hands are on Russell's shoulders.

He takes the cue, gets on his knees, and tries to get as much of Jeff's cock inside his inexperienced mouth.

Jeff watches Russell's ambitions. The heat of his mouth makes his feeble yet determined efforts on Jeff forgivable. Russell goes as deep as he can but then starts to gag so he pulls himself from the penis, but not before sending his teeth into the meat a few times. Jeff holds his head and helps him off his dick. After checking that no damage was done he holds his cock in front of Russell's mouth and rubs it gently over his lips. He then eases the head into his mouth, between his teeth. Russell closes his mouth over the cock, and Jeff, still holding his head still, gently fucks

Russell's mouth, giving him an idea of how a dick should be handled. Jeff moves them both to the couch, positions them in a sixty-nine, and initiates a game of monkey-*feel*-monkey-do.

Jeff is underneath Russell so that he is able at will to remove Russell's cock from his mouth and send his tongue into his ass. The feeling of tongue around his asshole sends Russell over the edge and he can no longer focus on Jeff's cock in his mouth. He frees his mouth so that he can make the noises necessary for him to refrain from climbing the walls. He is the equivalent of a chimpanzee crossed with a tiger on heat. Everything has Russell wanting to leap off of Jeff's face, but everything else keeps him there. Jeff eats out Russell's ass, determined to plant the seed that will have the very same ass swallow his cock in a minute.

Once the hole seems sufficiently wetted Jeff sends a cautious index in to explore. Now Russell jumps. Jeff is quick though and has a firm grip thrown around Russell's thighs almost at the waist, keeping him almost seated. He lets the finger in completely and then gives the young man a second before he is fucking the tight-as-hell asshole with the finger. It doesn't take too long for Russell to start screaming like a girl, asking to be fucked deeper and harder. Jeff tests the validity of these requests by adding another finger to the back-door assault. Russell's asshole is receptive.

After fucking the hole with two fingers for a while, Jeff reaches for a tube on the side table that Russell hadn't even seen before. The contents of the tube are cold on the area around Russell's hole as it coats the fingers that have made themselves at home inside him. Suddenly there is a strange new pressure on his anus, an added stretch that has him try to look back. But since he is practically sitting on Jeff's face, he can't see that Jeff has now added a third finger. Russell is pushed down towards the cock that has gone neglected too long and he manages to take it in his mouth, a welcome distraction now that his ass is being formally ripped apart.

Russell must be adapted to the finger fucking up his ass because suddenly his cock sucking is anything but amateur. He is pushing himself onto Jeff's hand while managing, thanks to his height; the full eleven inches that is Jeff's cock in his mouth. He has suddenly developed the ability to deep-throat and it is he who now has Jeff gasping. Jeff pushes Russell forward now so that he can part the ass cheeks with both his hands and give the hole a thorough inspection. It yawns and gapes at the slightest touch. This boy is ready to be fucked.

Jeff pulls Russell back onto his face for a final tonguing. The sensation has Russell sit up straight, Jeff sending practically his entire tongue into the once-was-tight hole. Occasionally Russell is able to reach forward and take Jeff's cock in his hands, milking it for as long as he can avoid pulling on his own dick in response to the slippery serpent shooting the greatest pleasure he's ever felt up the length of his spine. Jeff uses his tongue to coat the entrance of the asshole once more before lifting a fuck-ready Russell off of his face.

Russell is on his stomach, flat on the couch. Jeff manages a condom while drizzling just a few drops from the tube directly onto Russell's asshole. Suddenly the hole again seems tight and closed as Jeff tests it with his index. He forces the index in, Russell responding by stabbing his cock into the couch. Jeff gives the asshole a few more good jabs, circling the entrance in an attempt to widen it. He adds his middle finger, Russell now fucking the couch in an attempt to add a familiar pleasure to this new one. After giving him the time he needs to get lost in the couch-fucking Jeff sends his cock into him quickly, completely, impaling

Russell to the couch now. He grabs him under his arms and holds him in place as Russell lets out several subdued screams.

Slow strokes follow just as soon as the screaming becomes heavy breathing. This stroking brings on a new set of screams. Jeff knows to just keep going. He fucks the virgin with long deep strokes, Russell telling him repeatedly and in whispers that he was killing him. Jeff knows that he isn't, he knows that it won't be long now. His cock slides easily in and out of Russell thanks to the lube and so Jeff torments the boy a little more by removing his cock completely and stabbing it into him immediately. He does this a few times, driving Russell insane each time.

Eventually, Russell starts to follow Jeff up with his ass every time he thinks he might withdraw, clenching his ass muscles so that his hole has Jeff's cock in a chokehold. This is all the sign Jeff needs to know that it's all systems go.

There is nothing gentle now or careful, about the manner he fucks Russell. Jeff's thick cock is inside him deeper, harder than ever. He sends it to the boy repeatedly, Russell now gasping and begging for more all at once. Jeff responds with harder thrusts, sending his eleven inches so deep into Russell that his cock probably touches his navel. The fucking becomes fast and furious; a fierce ass pounding that fills the room with the sounds of super-savage sex. Russell's ass is no longer that of a virgin and so Jeff no longer treats it as such.

Jeff has his arms under Russell and lifts him up while he himself rises. He is careful not to let his cock escape from his ass. He gets onto his back so that Russell, still on his back, is now on top of him. This new position allows Russell to pull on his own cock while he is fucked from underneath. Jeff enjoys watching the boy beat his meat while his cock deals savage blows to his ass. Once he starts to see his own climax on the horizon though Jeff removes Russell's hands off his cock and takes the meat between his own thick fingers. He starts to jerk Russell off so expertly that Russell's ass starts to tighten more and more around his cock.

There is no time for Jeff to worry about where Russell's load will go as the perfect cylinder in his hand starts to spray cream all over the place. Russell is very loud about the pleasure he feels, Jeff is grateful that his living room is located in a part of the house that makes it extremely private. He doesn't try to silence his own orgasm either, the sight of the massive load coming from Russell inspiring his own ejaculation. His cock pulsates violently inside Russell's freshly deflowered rosebud, the condom barely able to keep the excessive semen contained. It takes them both a moment to process the super orgasms they've just had, but once breaths are caught, Russell is tipped generously before he disappears into the balmy afternoon.

ABOUT THE AUTHOR

Chaney Kees is an emerging erotica author of many erotica kinks and sub-genres. Be sure to check out other books and leave a review if this story got you hot!

Visit my blog at Chaney Kees's Blog

Join my newsletter for the exclusive Chaney Kees's Newsletter

Sign up for Free Stories from Xplicit Press AuthorsCandra Aubrey's Blog

Xplicit Press Author Updates

Like Xplicit Press on Facebook

Follow Xplicit Press on Twitter

Readers: I want to expand a few of the stories to see where the characters can be explored further. If there are any of the stories that you would like to read more about again, I'd love to hear from you!

Keep In Touch
Chaney Kees
info@chaneykees.com